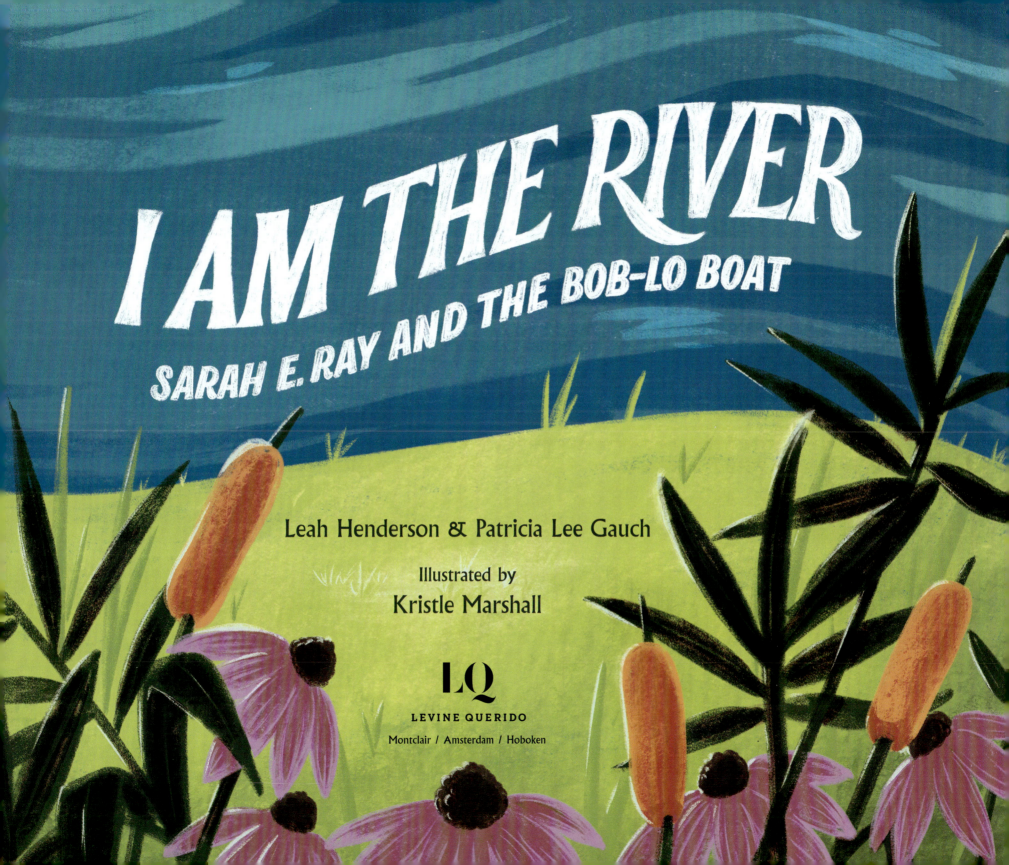

I AM THE RIVER

SARAH E. RAY AND THE BOB-LO BOAT

Leah Henderson & Patricia Lee Gauch

Illustrated by
Kristle Marshall

LQ
LEVINE QUERIDO

Montclair / Amsterdam / Hoboken

I am the river. Blue and green, fast and flowing, sweeping river grasses aside, racing fish like perch and bass, moving between Lake Erie and Detroit.

Canoes came first, birchbark arrows through my blue-green current,
then boats, sail and steam, carrying lumber and goods, steered,
or sailed, or steamed by river rat captains who talked tough.

Men and women came then, sometimes tugging
children, freedom seekers, escaped and running,
getting across to "the promised land."

I am the river boat captain who talked tough, plying the blue and green river, fast and sweeping. I am tough, but clear: These are men and women and sometimes children, running to be free. I understand living free.

"Get to the boats," I say, and men and women come, sometimes tugging children, wading into the river running blue and green, to board boats, the fresh and sweet smell of freedom in the wind. "I can get you there," I say. Hundreds of freedom seekers take my boats to Canada. But not all come this way.

I am the island in the blue and green river,
soldiered with white birch trees,
Bois Blanc (some hear "Bob-Lo"),
two and a half miles long, half a mile wide.

While tens and twenties board ships of captains
who understand freedom, and some come by the land itself,
so some stop here, then cross the river with dinghies and
skiffs and rafts—some swim—to Amherstburg, Canada.

I am a stepping-stone, one of the last on the
Underground Railroad.
Not a railroad at all but a string of secret houses
and stops running north from south.

I am a stepping-stone, one of the last, for men
and women, and sometimes whole precious
families crossing the river to freedom.

But time passes like the river,
and people forget.

I am the giant boat, one of two, called Bob-Lo, that plied the blue and green river from 1902, running fast. Five decks high with brass for railings and trombones blaring and popcorn popping, welcoming children from the city at the end of the river called Detroit.

In summers, they come escaping sweltering days. I am noisy, the engine turning, churning down the river to the same Bob-Lo Island, now a park of carousel and rides made of bright colored metal, a Wild Mouse, a Whip, and Ferris Wheel, and plinkety plink music soaring over the island, now cleared of birch trees.

I am the Bob-Lo boat, one of two.
Children love me. I know that.

But not all children—and not all adults—are welcome.

I am the city where the Bob-Lo boat begins its journey. Detroit. A city sprawling out from the blue and green river, factories with assembly lines a mile long, building cars, cars, cars, cars, cars, cars, cars.

Factories spouting smoke across the skies, and people flooding up from the South into the city by the river to work. No wonder people come in summers to the giant boats, to the island called Bob-Lo, where not all children and adults are welcome.

I am Sarah Elizabeth Ray, born in Tennessee. One of thirteen. A free soul with dreams. I'm not one for yes'um and no'um . . . uh-uh. I'm free much like the fast-flowing blue and green river. When I come of age, I journey upstream, past the Mason-Dixon Line, where I am supposed to be free. North, not south, to Detroit where jobs are aplenty, or so they say, and where education is open to me.

My classmates and teacher call for a celebration when secretarial school is complete.
A trip on a Bob-Lo boat to the Bob-Lo Island is where it's to be.

June 21, 1945. A summer's day. I'm ready for the ride. Money collected, ticket in hand, though the ticket taker—head down for all others—looks up when he sees me. All thirteen of us walk the plank. All thirteen of us board the giant boat, the S.S. *Columbia*, together. Coat checked, I take a seat near the railing, eager to see the river and park of carousel and rides, hear music soaring, plinkety plink.

A rowdy breeze bounces through the giant boat, five decks high, the blue and green river rocking and rustling below. The boat rumbles, engine turning, but it bobs, and bobs, and bobs against the dock—delayed. I'm nestled in, top deck, ready for the ride, when two men dressed in white come directly to me, and it is for no early prize.

"You will have to leave the boat," one says.

"Why?" I say. No coloreds on this boat is their reply.

Company rules. Boat rules. Definite rules.

The blue and green river plonks up against the sides of the giant boat, five decks high. While it plonks, I plonk too. No, no, no, no, no. I refuse. "Throw this woman off," they say. Three white waiters, ready to comply.

Before I push past the anger in my throat, my teacher speaks for me. "She'll go quietly," she says.

Wait! Those are not my words at all. And no words come from my twelve classmates, women I've clanked typewriter keys beside for months. Not one. Not one. Not one.

We *had* been the same. Wanted the same . . .
But not anymore.
Angry, and hurt, and humiliated, and embarrassed,
All of a sudden, I am different, I think.

Today, there is no promised land for me.

Thirteen boarded. Only one must go.

The two men at my side think the color of my skin, an enemy.

I leave the giant boat, five decks high, engine turning, ready to be set free.

On a journey not open to me. Not a stepping-stone on the Underground

Railroad now. No longer safe passage for those with skin the color of mine.

Back on Woodward Avenue Pier,
they return my fare. They do not want me.
They do not want my money. My eighty-five cents.
I throw it at the boat. I do not want it either!
But I do want justice.

I stop at the first phone box I see.

I slide a nickel into the slot and make the call I need.

It is the NAACP, the National Association for the Advancement of Colored People, who answer the call. Hear my insult, my anger, my humiliation. My need to fight.

And fight we do in a lawsuit against the Bob-Lo Excursion Company. Michigan law states loud and clear: Discrimination on any public conveyance is illegal. Bob-Lo Company has violated my civil rights!

At a local Michigan court (we win!); at the Michigan Supreme Court (we win!); and finally, finally to the highest court in the land: the United States Supreme Court, argued by a passionate young man named Thurgood Marshall (we win, we win!).

Bob-Lo Boat Ban Illegal

Excurs
Guilty i
Rights

And Sarah Elizabeth Ray wins too.

As constant as the blue and green river, fast and flowing, Sarah Elizabeth was constant in her belief that right was right and fair was fair.

Over time, the Bob-Lo boat welcomed *all* children and adults, of every color, chugging down the river to the island full of play.

Sarah Elizabeth could have, but she chose not to step back on the giant boat, five decks high, brass railings sparkling, trombones blaring.

She could have, but she chose not to ever visit the island where the carousel, Wild Mouse, Whip, and Ferris Wheel stood and plinkety plink music soared over the land.

But there was a fire in Sarah Elizabeth, and whenever she had the opportunity to act, and to do, and to remember, she did. And throughout her life, she continued to listen to and speak for the voices sometimes seen, but not always heard.

I AM THE AUTHOR (PATTI)

I was obsessed with the Bob-Lo boats. Growing up near Lake St. Clair, I lived close enough to hear hollow freighters' horns at night. I saw boats of every kind motoring or sailing toward or away from Detroit. But there was nothing like the Bob-Lo boats for me, the two five-tiered wedding-cake steamboats that plied the Detroit River during the summer, taking children and families eighteen miles downriver to Bob-Lo (Bois Blanc) Island and the noisy, colorful amusement park there.

Everyone, it seemed, loved the Bob-Lo boats, at times thousands crowding onto their decks, from the time the boats began their runs in 1902 until 1993, when the boats disappeared. As an adult, I returned to Michigan from the East and discovered them gone. The Detroit piers and river, empty. But where did they go, and why? My heart ached from the loss.

I searched relentlessly, discovering through newspaper and online articles and photographs that in recent times attendance had sadly fallen off, and in 1993 the two boats had been retired and moored in downriver Ecorse, their once beautiful decks and brass railing staircases and fairytale dance floor deteriorating.

But in searching for the missing boats, I stumbled upon stories, not only of the boats, but of the river, the boundary between Canada and the United States; it was a line of safety for the formerly enslaved freedom seekers from the mid-nineteenth-century South. Amherstburg, a five-minute ferry ride across the river from Bob-Lo Island, was said to be the end of the Underground Railroad. How was it that, growing up as close to the lakes and river as I did, I had never heard this story in any of my worlds, including my family, my classrooms, nowhere? Somehow this crucial but amazing story was lost to me.

But another story lost to me and other Detroiters, this one from a century later, was very disturbing . . .

I AM THE AUTHOR TOO (LEAH)

When Patti shared the histories she'd uncovered with me, I was fascinated and immediately wanted to help her dig deeper. To explore the story that had hardly been told. To hear Sarah Elizabeth Ray's words, to admire her bravery, and to recognize her role in a larger story. While I was unfamiliar with the Bob-Lo boats and Sarah Elizabeth's actions, I was not unfamiliar with her feelings of frustration, not only at how she had been treated, but at how her story and so many others have gone unheard. As Patti observed, they were left out of school history books, classroom discussions, and family conversations. And in some small way, I wanted to help this particular history be heard.

How could a story that helped lay the groundwork for future civil rights cases go forgotten?

Ten years before Rosa Parks refused to give up her seat on a Montgomery bus, a young Sarah Elizabeth Ray, shunned by her classmates and teachers, refused to stay silent in the face of a company's prejudice and injustice. What kind of courage did that take? I wanted to know, and I also wanted to learn more about how the esteemed Thurgood Marshall took this case all the way to the Supreme Court and won. A case that no doubt helped to inform his litigation in the 1954 Supreme Court case *Brown v. Board of Education of Topeka*, which ended segregation in schools and led to desegregation based on color for the nation.

Like in a river, one action can have a ripple effect, and Sarah's actions did. Ripples that affected not only her and the Bob-Lo Excursion Company but in years to come the entire nation.

Hers is a story we hope will always be remembered.

For freedom seekers of every time and place —P.L.G.

For those whose unsung stories have yet to be shared —L.H.

It has been an honor to become immersed in this historical moment, which has surely shaped the legacy of Detroit and my freedoms as a Black woman living and growing in the Greater Detroit community. May the story of Sarah E. Ray be an inspiration for many generations. —K.M.

SELECTED SOURCES

Bob-Lo Excursion Co. v. People of Michigan (U.S. Supreme Court decision), Feb. 2, 1948, https://www.law.cornell.edu/supremecourt/text/333/28.

Cooper, Desiree. "Long Journey Ends Injustice." *Detroit Free Press*, Feb. 28, 2006, pp. 1B, 7B.

Quammie, Bee. "Freedom Ships and the Little-Known History of the Resistance" (segment 5 of CBC documentary series *Enslaved*), last updated Nov. 9, 2020, https://www.cbc.ca/documentaries/enslaved/freedom-ships-and-the-little-known-history-of-resistance-1.5786441.

Rye, Clayton. "Rosa Parks of the Bob-Lo Boats" (interview with Sarah Elizabeth Haskell). YouTube, Sept. 9, 2020, https://www.youtube.com/watch?v=0-NL832flk4.

Soodalter, Ron. "All Aboard: The Fight Against Segregation on Bob-Lo Island." *The Progressive Magazine*, June 1, 2016, https://progressive.org/magazine/aboard-fight-segregation-bob-lo-island-soodalter/.

This is an Arthur A. Levine book
Published by Levine Querido

LQ
LEVINE QUERIDO

www.levinequerido.com • info@levinequerido.com
Levine Querido is distributed by Chronicle Books, LLC
Text copyright © 2026 by Patricia Lee Gauch and Leah Henderson
Illustration copyright © 2026 by Kristle Marshall

Library of Congress Control Number: 2024951023

ISBN 978-1-64614-580-5
Printed and bound in China

FSC
www.fsc.org
MIX
Paper | Supporting
responsible forestry
FSC™ C008047

Published January 2026
First Printing

Book design by Cara Llewellyn
The text type was set in Albertus MT and the display type was handlettered by Kristle Marshall.
The artwork for this picture book began with pencil and paper, and was rendered digitally
with pen and tablet in Procreate and Adobe Photoshop.